Duff the Giant Killer

Illustrations by Kim LaFave

FIRST NOVELS

The New Series

Formac Publishing Limited
Halifax, Nova Scotia

Formac Publishing Company Limited acknowledges the support of The Canada Council and the Nova Scotia Department of Education and Culture in the development of writing and publishing in Canada.

Canadian Cataloguing in Publication Data

Wilson, Budge

Duff the giant killer

(First novel series)

ISBN 0-88780-382-2 (pbk.) ISBN 0-88780-383-0 (bound)

I. LaFave, Kim II. Title. III. Series.

PS8595.I5813D84 1997 jC813'.54 C96-950224-9
PZ7.W69004Du 1997

Formac Publishing Limited
5502 Atlantic Street
Halifax, N.S. B3H 1G4

Printed and bound in Canada.

Contents

To my friend
Alice Nicholl

1
An Early Start

Duff woke up early on that Thursday morning. He opened his eyes and ran his fingers through his untidy mop of red hair. It always looked as though he'd just come in from a wind storm. He went downstairs to the front hall and dialed Simon's number.

Mrs. Abrams answered the phone, her voice foggy and frosty. "Hello," she said. She sounded as though she were speaking through a bundle of cotton wool.

"I want to speak to Simon,

please," said Duff, very cheerfully, very politely.

"Do you know what time it is, Duff?" asked Mrs. Abrams' weary voice.

"No," he said, straining his neck to look out the window. Well, it did seem to be kind of dark.

"Five-thirty," Simon's mother said. "Five twenty-two to be exact. I got to bed at two-thirty, after feeding the baby. It would be nice to get some sleep. And no, you can't speak to Simon. Like every other sensible person in Peterborough, he's sound asleep."

"No, he's not!" yelled a voice from the stairway. Simon was taking the steps three at a time. Thunk! Thunk! Thunk! on the hardwood stairs. Duff could hear him right through the phone.

"No hope of getting back to sleep *now*," groaned Mrs. Abrams, dropping the receiver on the hall table.

Duff heard the clunk of the phone as it landed.

"Hey! Simon!" he shouted. "Are you there?" Duff had never learned that a telephone can carry your voice, even if you're not shrieking.

"Yeah," answered Simon. "Sure, I'm here. Where else would I be?"

Duff was still yelling. "Are you busy?"

"No. No, I'm not busy. Why would I be busy at five-thirty in the morning?"

"Look, Simon," said Duff. "I've got stuff I have to do till ten o'clock—the dentist and all. How about you meet me up by Clonsilla Avenue at five after? We'll have ourselves a time."

"Great!" said Simon. "See you later, alligator."

Duff replaced the phone and looked up at the top of the stairs. His whole family was standing there—all of them in their pyjamas. Not one of them looked friendly.

"What on earth are you *doing*?" said his father. It wasn't really a question.

"You must be out of your tree to be making phone calls at this hour!" growled his sister, rubbing her eyes with the heel of her hand. "And why can't you—

for once in your life—make a *quiet* call?"

Mrs. Dooley just looked up at the ceiling and muttered, "I give up. I don't deserve this."

Duff ignored all their sleepy faces. "Gee!" he said. "I can't meet Simon till I'm through with the dentist. And my appointment isn't until nine. What'll I do with all that empty time?"

Mrs. Dooley sighed. "You could maybe try sleeping," she said, as she staggered back to the bedroom.

2
Convalescing

Four-and-a-half hours later, Duff Dooley and Simon Abrams were crossing Clonsilla Avenue. Duff's shaggy red hair clashed with his face full of orange freckles. Simon had black eyes with hair to match. They were best friends. They spent so much time together that when Duff had chicken pox, Simon got it a week later. ("Just like Duff to get it first," Simon had complained.) By now, the itching had stopped and the spots were almost gone. But they weren't allowed to go on the class bus trip to the Science Centre. They were convalescing instead.

"What's 'convalescing'?" asked Simon, as they walked down Sherbrooke Avenue and turned onto Albertus.

Duff had all the answers to most questions. So he replied right away. "Convalescing," he said, "is when you've been sick but aren't germy anymore. You can't go to school, which is okay, but you can't go on any school trips either, which is *not* okay. Convalescing is when you're bored right out of your skull."

"Never mind," said Simon. "Even if we're convalescing, I bet you can think of something neat to do. Let's go over to Hastings Park and swing on the equipment until you get a brain wave."

"A brain wave," said Duff, "is when you get an idea that's so spectacular that it almost blows you over."

"I *know* that, dummy," said Simon. "It was me that said it."

Duff was fun—the most fun person that Simon had ever known. But he sure was pushy.

* * *

Over at the Abrams' house, Mrs. Dooley and Mrs. Abrams were having a cup of coffee. Duff's mother had a part-time job in the afternoon, but right now it was morning. Mrs. Abrams was feeding squashed bananas to the baby—Simon's sister, Rachel.

"Babies are easy," said Mrs. Abrams (forgetting altogether that Rachel had wakened her up three times last night). "It's those two eight-year-old boys who can sometimes drive you wild."

"Fun, though," chuckled Mrs. Dooley. She was wearing a pair of faded jeans, and her wild red hair (just like Duff's) was tied back with a bright green bandana. She put her feet up on Mrs. Abrams' coffee table and grinned. "Always dreaming up some crazy scheme. Full of imagination."

"Too much, sometimes," said Mrs. Abrams. "Remember the time they knocked over poor old Mrs. Pitski when they were pretending to be a herd of buffalos?"

They both laughed. Nobody seemed to be remembering the five-thirty phone call. "But good kids," said Mrs. Dooley. "They never get into any *real* trouble."

3
The Giant Killer

Duff and Simon were the only people in Hastings Park. For a while they pretended to be monkeys and chimpanzees, as they climbed (upside down and right side up) on the jungle gym. But soon they got tired of being monkeys. Then they tried the swings, but that didn't seem to work either.

"How about being space aliens?" suggested Simon.

"Dull city," said Duff. "We did that yesterday. Never do the same thing two days in a row."

"Right," said Simon. "Especially not have a bath." He laughed. "I'd better tell Mom about that rule."

"Think!" ordered Duff. "I don't see any brain waves coming off these swings."

They swung in silence for a while, pretending to be trapeze artists, parachute troops, balloonists.

"I've got it!" yelled Duff.

"Yeah?" Simon jumped off the swing. "What?"

"You know that cartoon we saw last week on TV—*Jack the Giant-Killer*?"

"Yeah."

"Well—let's make our own play. We can go over to the school yard and put it on at the bottom of the big hill that goes up to Grandview Avenue. Let's

pretend the hill is our audience. We can do the play on the flat part. It'll be our stage."

"Great brain wave!" said Simon, slapping Duff on the back.

"You get to be the giant," said Duff, "because you're tall. I'll be the killer. Because I'm so tough. But we'll change the story. C'mon…let's get going. We'll talk about the plot on the way over."

If you ran, it usually only took four minutes to get to the school yard from Hastings Park. This time they were there in three and three-quarter minutes, just as the kids poured back into the school after recess.

"We'll have the whole place to ourselves," grinned Duff, pushing back his tangled red hair with his grimy fingers.

They sank down, panting, on the warm grass. Sometimes May can be almost hot, and this was one of those days. It would have been nice to go swimming, but you can't swim if you're convalescing from chicken pox.

No. It had to be Jack the Giant-Killer. Or better still, Duff the Giant-Killer.

4
The Tragedy Unfolds

"Okay," said Simon, digging Duff in the ribs. "How'll we change the play?"

Duff was lying on his back with his arms linked behind his head. He was chewing on a piece of grass and trying not to get his gum tangled up in it.

Simon gnawed on his bottom lip for a moment. "We could make the giant kill *Jack*, I suppose," he muttered.

"No," said Duff. He spat out both grass and gum in a mushy pink and green wad. "That's too easy. The giant's so huge. We need a long and very fierce fight. With swords."

They jumped up and went off to search for sticks that would be big enough to use as swords.

"Hey!" cried Duff. "I know! The giant can be in disguise. Or someone put a spell on him or something, and he's really Jack's best friend."

"Great!" said Simon. "So, even during the big fight, and even when the giant gets hit in the heart, Jack still doesn't know the real truth."

"But *then*," continued Duff, who was liking his idea better every minute, "at the moment when life slowly starts to trickle out of the giant, he changes back into who he really is—Jack's closest, dearest, life-long friend."

"Then," said Simon, "we'll have a sad scene while the giant is dying. He'll be saying—no, he'll be *gasping*—pathetic things about their being friends forever. His voice'll be all choked up and raspy."

"And Jack'll be like a wild person, beating his head with grief and sorrow!" Duff starting beating his own head. He could hardly wait to get started.

"It'll be a *very* sad play," he said. "A TRAGEDY!"

They finally found sticks that made good swords, and brought them back to their stage at the foot of the hill. Now they were almost ready.

But first they needed some make-up. Duff reached down and dug out a handful of earth from under the grass. He spat on it again and again until it became mud. Then he rubbed it on Simon's face, making him look fierce and evil. He was a lot taller than Duff, so he'd make a good giant. Duff took off his sweater and tied it around his neck for a cape. He was glad it was red. It looked good with his green T-shirt.

5
Mrs. Fogo Gets Worried

Mrs. Fogo looked out of her kitchen window on Grandview Avenue and admired her view. She loved to enjoy the lights of the city after dark and to see the sun rise in the morning.

But most of all, she liked watching the kids in the school yard racing around during recess, playing all their games, and doing their crazy kid things. Her own children were grown up and had moved far away to British Columbia. She was happy that she could still see lots of children and enjoy the fun they had.

Now, what were those two boys doing in the school yard during school hours? Playing hookey? Should she call the school? Well...maybe not. She could recall the time her own daughter had skipped school, and someone had reported her to the principal. Mrs. Fogo had been *so mad*. Millicent had had detentions for a whole week, and had been late for her own birthday party. No, she wouldn't call the principal. But she'd watch.

The one with the filthy dirty face looked like a real bully. And he had a stick which he was pointing at the smaller boy. Mrs. Fogo always hated it when kids played with sticks. So dangerous. You could hit someone in the eye and blind them. But small

boys seemed to think they just had to have sticks for poking at people and swinging around. Girls were different. Well…not always. She tried not to remember the time she'd hit her best friend with a stick after she'd broken her favourite doll, when they'd both been six years old. Some things are best forgotten.

Those boys looked to be about eight. Maybe nine. The one with the red hair was waving his arms around as though he was having a big argument with the bully.

Oh, dear. A fight. And they *both* had sticks. Worse and worse. They began heaving them around and slapping them together. If they didn't soon stop, someone was going to get hurt. Even from here, she could see how angry they both were.

6
Call 911!

Mrs. Fogo went out onto her front porch. She wanted to get a better view of the fight. In fact, she brought along her husband's binoculars so that she could be sure of what she was seeing.

Oh! They were definitely fighting. The red-headed one was smaller, but he seemed very quick and ferocious, maybe even tougher and stronger than the big one—and definitely *mean*. Not that she blamed him. But why couldn't people be peaceful? It was so much nicer. No wonder there were so many wars.

The dirty-faced one seemed to be weakening. Serves him right for starting it, thought Mrs. Fogo. The red-head shoved him hard—really HARD—with the stick, and down he went. He raised himself up on his elbow for a moment, as though pleading for mercy, but he seemed to be losing strength. Finally, after one last hoarse cry (she could hear him very clearly), he slumped down, eyes closed.

Mrs. Fogo put down her binoculars for a moment, wondering what she should do. She watched the red-headed boy rushing over to Dirty Face, kneeling down to look at him. His fist flew up to his mouth, as though in horror. Then he put his head down on the other

boy's chest. *Why? To listen to his breathing?* Or to see if he *WAS* breathing? Mrs. Fogo's heart was thudding like a drum inside her ribs.

Suddenly Red Head threw his arms up towards the sky and started to howl. She could hear him as plainly as if he'd been in the next room.

"My friend!" he was yelling. "My best and only true friend! Dead! Dead! Dead! I've *KILLED* him!"

Even with her heart almost jumping out of her chest, Mrs. Fogo now knew exactly what she should do. She turned around, leaving the binoculars carelessly on the front steps, and hurried into the house. Going straight to the phone, she lifted the receiver and dialled 911.

"Get me the police department," she said. "And FAST!"

7
The Police Get Set

Down at the police station it had been a dull morning. No murders. No burglars. No purse snatchings. Not even any barking dogs to be dealt with. Nothing except paper work to catch up on, lunch to be served to the one prisoner in the jail, a lot of cups of lukewarm coffee to be drunk. Not a very interesting day. One of the officers started to yawn as he leafed through a pile of court reports.

Suddenly the phone rang, right in the middle of the officer's yawn. The voice at the other end was both squeaky and frantic. He could only catch about every third word: "...terrible fight...before my very eyes ...severely wounded... maybe even DEAD. Come at once!"

Two of the officers rose and strapped their guns onto their waists.

"What do you think?" said one.

"Looks bad," said the other. "Very bad."

"Juvenile homicide. Nothing worse. But he could still be alive. Better call the ambulance."

The second officer dialed swiftly. "Quick!" he said. "Corner of Monaghan and Sherbrooke, school yard, west side. A kid. If

POLICE STATION
ZZZZ
CAPT.

you hurry, he might still be alive. But I doubt it. Bring oxygen. And all the emergency gear. Meet you there."

8
Trouble!

Over in the school yard, Duff was still waving his arms around, howling with grief and remorse. Simon lay still as a stone, eyes closed, arms folded across his chest. Duff got down on the blacktop on all fours, beating the ground with his fist.

"My friend! My friend!" he cried. "Killed by my very own hand!"

Then the corpse opened his eyes and looked around. "Great play!" he said, grinning with satisfaction. "Way better than the show on TV."

Then the boys collapsed on the ground—flat on their stomachs—shrieking with laughter. To Duff's ears, the shrieking sounded unusually loud.

"Wait!" he said to Simon. "Stop laughing. Listen! Sirens—more than one! We may be missing a great fire. Or maybe a bank robbery. Let's see where they're going." They raised their heads.

Where they were going was right into the school yard. Duff and Simon looked on in amazement, as a police car sped into the parking area, followed by a large ambulance. Doors flew open and two officers dashed towards them, while the ambulance paramedics raced across the yard with their stretcher.

Mrs. Fogo was close behind them, pressing her chest to slow down her heart, her apron flapping in the wind.

Slowly Duff and Simon turned over and sat up.

"Which is the one who's supposed to be dying?" said one of the paramedics from the ambulance, hauling out his stethoscope.

"The dirty one," said Mrs. Fogo, feeling uneasy. How could that big boy be so dead one moment and so alive the next?

Simon's pulse was taken. His heart was listened to. He had to open his mouth and say "Ah!"

"This kid," said the paramedic, "is far healthier than I am." Then he turned to the police officers.

"Officers," he said, "I think this is your territory, not ours. We're not often called to come out and rescue a 100 percent healthy person."

One of the officers stepped forward and took out a notebook.

"Names!" he said.

"Duff Dooley."

"Simon Abrams."

"Were you fighting?"

"No," said Duff. "Playing."

"Huh!" sniffed Mrs. Fogo. "Killing each other is more like it."

The officer frowned. "Please," he said. "We can handle this ourselves, Mrs. Fogo."

"Okay, kids," said the other officer. "What exactly were you doing?"

"Putting on a play," said Duff. "*Jack the Giant-Killer*. I was the killer." Duff folded his arms across his chest, looking as though he could kill any number of giants. Or police officers, for that matter.

"Why were you shouting that he was dead?"

"Because he was."

"Why were you saying, 'My *friend* is dead!' "

"Because the giant wasn't really a giant. He was a friend. Because of ..." Duff stopped. This was too complicated.

"Because of what?"

"Because of the evil spell."

The officer looked up at the sky, and then he put his note-book back in his pocket. He sighed. "Get in the car, kids.

We'll all go down to the station and talk some more about this. If you're going to scare the wits out of your neighbours, I think we need to give you boys something to worry about, too. We'll take your fingerprints and get some mug shots."

9
Two Scared Mothers

Mrs. Abrams and Mrs. Dooley were having a pleasant morning. Rachel had been put to bed, and was actually sleeping. Mrs. Abrams put on a fresh pot of coffee, and got out her tin of chocolate chip cookies. Then they went back to their favourite topic: Duff and Simon.

"Yes," said Mrs. Dooley, "we've often wondered if the boys'll ever settle down and do anything sensible. Our house is just chock full of things that aren't really there. Like spacemen and gorillas and masked bandits."

"Oh, I know, I *know*," laughed Mrs. Abrams. "Our house, too. Crocodiles in the bathtub, sabre-toothed tigers in the backyard, aliens in the attic. Never a dull moment—or a peaceful one."

"But also never anything really *bad*," said Duff's mother.

"Oh, absolutely not. Never a single thing we need to worry about," agreed Mrs. Abrams.

Then the phone rang. Simon's mother lifted the receiver.

"Hello," she said.

"Hello, ma'am," said a man's voice. "This is the police department, Constable Curtis speaking. You Mrs. Abrams? Are you Simon's mother?"

Mrs. Abrams could feel her ribs expanding with the terror that was inside her. *Simon!* In an

accident? In the hospital?

Or...worse?

"Yes," she said. "Is...?"

"We couldn't locate Duff Dooley's mother," continued the voice. "We need her, too. Do you know where we could reach her?"

Mrs. Abrams couldn't speak. She just handed the phone to Mrs. Dooley. She watched as her friend's face collapsed, revealing exactly the same fears she was feeling.

"Yes," said Mrs. Dooley, her hand shaking, her coffee slurping over the side of the mug. "But is..."

"The boys are at the station," said the officer. "We've taken their fingerprints, but we need you both to come down and sign a statement."

Mrs. Dooley put the phone back on the table and looked at Mrs. Abrams.

"Never anything really *bad*," she said.

"And never a single thing we need to worry about," said Mrs. Abrams.

10
After the Storm

The boys were very quiet and serious that evening. At Duff's house, Mr. Dooley told Duff how fed up he was with the way his imagination seemed to be out of control.

"But…" said Duff.

"I mean it," said his father.

His mother said, "That poor Mrs. Fogo might have had a heart attack."

"I'm sorry," said Duff.

* * *

Two streets over, things weren't any better at the Abrams' house.

Mr. Abrams sat down opposite Simon at the kitchen table and said, "Look, Simon, couldn't you and Duff maybe do something normal and ordinary for a change—like read, or play ball, or even watch TV—instead of all the crazy things you're always doing?"

"But..." said Simon. He was thinking about how it had all started out as Duff's idea.

"But nothing," said Mr. Abrams, with a fierce frown. "You scared your mother half to death."

"I'm sorry," said Simon.

* * *

The next day, Duff met Simon again at the swing set.

"We sure got ourselves in a

big mess yesterday," said Duff.

"Yeah!" said Simon. "You can say *that* again!"

"Mad!" said Duff. "They were *both* mad."

"Same here," said Simon. "Even the baby cried at the police station."

"*But*..." began Duff—and let out a big laugh.

"I know," said Simon.

"Wasn't it something special to see that ambulance and that police car come racing into the school yard? For *us*? Acting like I'd *murdered* you? Ever neat!" Duff closed his eyes at the thought, and grinned. His freckles looked unusually bright.

"And down at the police station! Getting fingerprinted.

Having our pictures taken and all. Pretty awesome. I bet the kids at school won't even believe it." Simon sighed.

"Well," said Duff, "they don't believe much that we tell them, anyway. I mean about the aliens and tigers and UFOs and stuff."

Simon smiled. "Never mind. It'll be something to tell our grandchildren. A real live adventure. We can leave out the part about the angry parents."

"Yeah," agreed Duff. "I can just hear those kids saying, 'Wow! It sure must have been exciting, 'way back when Grandpa was a kid!'"

Simon looked over at Duff. "So...what'll we do this afternoon?"

"Well," said Duff, "I was

thinking we might go down to the mall and hunt for foreign spies. Good plan?"

Simon stared at Duff and shook his head. He sure could dream up great ideas with the speed of light.

"Let's go!" he yelled.

Which is exactly what they did.

A Note from the Author

The story of Duff and Simon is based on an incident in a book I wrote several years ago and which is now out of print, titled *Going Bananas*. Now that you know Duff and Simon, I hope you will look for another book about them, which we're calling *Duff's Monkey Business*. This time Duff and Simon get themselves into an even bigger mess. It will be published in this same series, and it's actually my original story — in a slightly revised form.

Meet five other great kids in the New First Novels Series:

- **Meet Morgan the Magician**
  in *Morgan Makes Magic*
  by Ted Staunton/Illustrated by Bill Slavin
  When he's in a tight spot, Morgan tells stories — and most of them stretch the truth, to say the least. But when he tells kids at his new school he can do magic tricks, he really gets in trouble — most of all with the dreaded Aldeen Hummel!

- **Meet Jan the Curious**
  in *Jan's Big Bang*
  by Monica Hughes/Illustrated by Carlos Friere
  Taking part in the Science Fair is a big deal for Grade Three kids, but Jan and her best friend Sarah are ready for the challenge. Still, finding a safe project isn't easy, and the girls discover that getting ready for the fair can cause a whole lot of trouble.

- **Meet Robyn the Dreamer**
  in *Shoot for the Moon, Robyn*
  by Hazel Hutchins/ Illustrated by Yvonne Cathcart
  When the teacher asks her to sing for the class, Robyn knows it's her chance to be

the world's best singer. Should she perform like Celine Dion, or do *My Bonnie Lies Over the Ocean*, or the matchmaker song? It's hard to decide, even for the world's best singer — and the three boys who throw spitballs don't make it any easier.

- **Meet Carrie the Courageous in** *Go For It, Carrie*

by Lesley Choyce/ Illustrated by Mark Thurman

More than anything else, Carrie wants to roller-blade. Her big brother and his friend just laugh at her. But Carrie knows she can do it if she just keeps trying. As her friend Gregory tells her, "You can do it, Carrie. Go for it!"

- **Meet Lilly the Bossy in** *Lilly to the Rescue*

by Brenda Bellingham/ Illustrated by Kathy Kaulbach

Bossy-boots! That's what kids at school start calling Lilly when she gives a lot of advice that's not wanted. Lilly can't help telling people what to do — but how can she keep any of her friends if she always knows better?

Look for these First Novels!

- ***About Arthur***
  Arthur Throws a Tantrum
  Arthur's Dad
  Arthur's Problem Puppy

- ***About Fred***
  Fred and the Stinky Cheese
  Fred's Dream Cat

- ***About the Loonies***
  Loonie Summer
  The Loonies Arrive

- ***About Maddie***
  Maddie in Hospital
  Maddie Goes to Paris
  Maddie in Danger
  Maddie in Goal
  Maddie Wants Music
  That's Enough Maddie!

- ***About Mikey***
  Good For You, Mikey Mite!
  Mikey Mite Goes to School
  Mikey Mite's Big Problem

- ***About Mooch***
  Mooch Forever
  Hang On, Mooch!
  Mooch Gets Jealous
  Mooch and Me

- ***About the Swank Twins***
  The Swank Prank
  Swank Talk

- ***About Max***
  Max the Superhero
